3-D ART SKILLS LAB

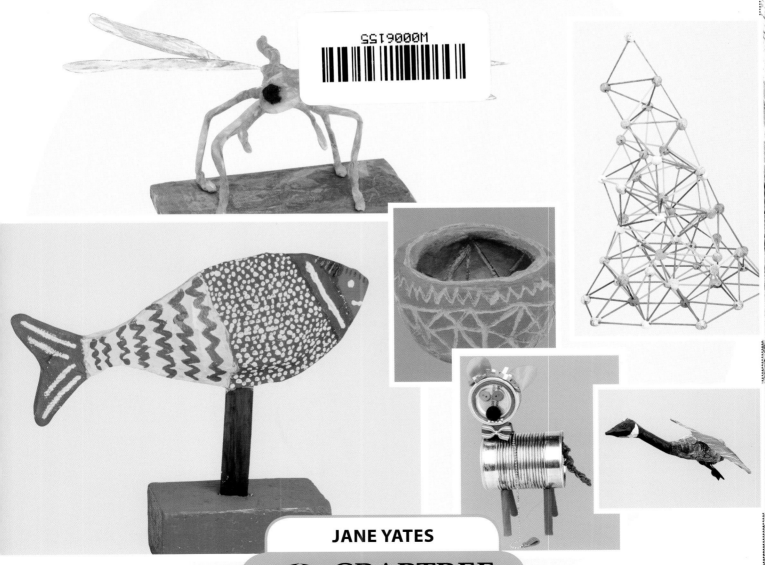

JANE YATES

CRABTREE
PUBLISHING COMPANY
WWW.CRABTREEBOOKS.COM

ART SKILLS LAB

Author
Jane Yates

Editors
Marcia Abramson, Reagan Miller

Photo research
Melissa McClellan

Cover/Interior Design
T.J. Choleva

Project Designer
Jane Yates

Proofreader
Crystal Sikkens

**Production coordinator
and Prepress technician**
Tammy McGarr

Print coordinator
Katherine Berti

Developed and produced for
Crabtree Publishing by
BlueApple*Works* Inc.

Consultant
Trevor Hodgson
Fine artist and former director of The Dundas Valley School of Art

Art & Photographs
Shutterstock.com: © Yulia elf_inc Tropina (cover middle left); © Excellent backgrounds (background); © Elena Yakusheva (p. 4 left); © Claudiovidri/Shutterstock.com (p. 4 right); © Jiri Hera (p. 5 middle left); © Brian Kenney/Shutterstock.com (p. 5 bottom left); © Ilike (p. 6 bottom); © JHVEPhoto/Shutterstock.com (p. 15 bottom right); alionabirukova/Shutterstock.com (p. 19 bottom left); © Rudy Mareel/Shutterstock.com (p. 21 right); © gvictoria/Shutterstock.com (p. 23 top right); © Rosalba Lopez (p. 25 top right); © optimarc (p. 25 bottom right); © Mark Rooks (p. 28 bottom);

© Austen Photography (cover, title page, TOC, p. 6 top, p. 7, p. 8– 29)

Instructive sculptures © Jane Yates cover, p. 7– 29 excluding bios

p. 5 top Auguste Rodin/Metropolitan Museum of Art/Creative Commons
p. 5 top left Qaunaq Mikkigak (Cape Dorset, Nunavut Territory, Canada)
p. 5 bottom right Lubo Kristek/Creative Commons
p. 9 right Metropolitan Museum of Art/Creative Commons
p. 11 Metropolitan Museum of Art/Public Domain
p. 13 bottom right Gniw/Public Domain
p. 17 bottom right/Public Domain
p. 19 bottom right GFDL/Creative Commons
p. 27 bottom right Shrewdcat/Creative Commons
p. 29 bottom right Hans Bug /Creative Commons

Library and Archives Canada Cataloguing in Publication

Yates, Jane, author
        3-D art skills lab / Jane Yates.

(Art skills lab)
Includes index.
Issued in print and electronic formats.
ISBN 978-0-7787-5219-6 (hardcover).--
ISBN 978-0-7787-5225-7 (softcover).--
ISBN 978-1-4271-2176-9 (HTML)

        1. Sculpture--Technique--Juvenile literature. 2. Sculpture--
Juvenile literature. I. Title. II. Title: Three-D art skills lab.

NB1170.Y38 2018   j731.4   C2018-905544-8
                                                                    C2018-905545-6

Library of Congress Cataloging-in-Publication Data

Names: Yates, Jane, author.
Title: 3-D art skills lab / Jane Yates.
Other titles: Three-D art skills lab
Description: New York, New York : Crabtree Publishing Company,
    [2019] |
Series: Art skills lab | Includes index.
Identifiers: LCCN 2018050800 (print) | LCCN 2018057003 (ebook) |
    ISBN 9781427121769 (Electronic) |
    ISBN 9780778752196 (hardcover : alk. paper) |
    ISBN 9780778752257 (pbk. : alk. paper)
Subjects: LCSH: Sculpture--Technique--Juvenile literature. |
    Mixed media (Art)--Technique--Juvenile literature.
Classification: LCC NB1143 (ebook) | LCC NB1143 .Y38 2019 (print) |
    DDC 730.28--dc23
LC record available at https://lccn.loc.gov/2018050800

Crabtree Publishing Company

www.crabtreebooks.com   1-800-387-7650

Printed in the U.S.A./012019/CG20181123

**Published in Canada
Crabtree Publishing**
616 Welland Ave.
St. Catharines, Ontario
L2M 5V6

**Published in the United States
Crabtree Publishing**
PMB 59051
350 Fifth Avenue, 59th Floor
New York, New York 10118

**Published in the United Kingdom
Crabtree Publishing**
Maritime House
Basin Road North, Hove
BN41 1WR

**Published in Australia
Crabtree Publishing**
Unit 3 – 5 Currumbin Court
Capalaba
QLD 4157

CONTENTS

GET INTO 3-D ART

Approach this book with a sense of adventure! It is designed to unleash the creativity that exists within you! The projects in this book will help you express your feelings, your thoughts, and your ideas through your art. Create images of things you want to say, and messages you want to share. When learning to make 3-D art, enjoy the process and don't worry too much about the finished product. To make it easier, all the clay projects in this book can be created without a **kiln**. Find your own individual style and run with it!

MINI-BIOGRAPHIES

Throughout the book you will find mini-biographies highlighting the work of well-known artists. You can learn a lot about 3-D **techniques** by looking at great works of art. Experiment with the techniques the artists used. Examine each artwork to see how its parts were put together, then put your own touch into creating art.

WHAT IS 3-D ART

Objects have height, width, and depth, which are called **dimensions**. When artwork has all three, it's called three-dimensional or 3-D art. Paintings and photos have height and width but not depth, so they are two-dimensional. Artists and filmmakers can use special techniques to achieve a 3-D effect on a flat surface, but that is not 3-D art. Clay, metal, wood, rocks, and even found objects can be used to make 3-D art. They can be as small as a coffee mug or as large as a giant sculpture in a public plaza.

Large sculptures can be designed by the artist, but the actual construction is done by many people. The Chicago Picasso, a very large metal sculpture by Pablo Picasso in Chicago, Illinois, is a great example of this.

MAIN TYPES OF 3-D ART

3-D art can fall in to one of many categories:

ADDITIVE SCULPTURE

Additive sculpture is when material is added to create a form. It can be made with clay, wax, plaster, or papier-mâché.

A **terracotta** sculpture created by Auguste Rodin in 1891 is an example of additive sculpting.

SUBTRACTIVE SCULPTURE

Subtractive sculpture is creating a 3-D piece of art by removing material. It is usually made by carving wood or stone such as marble, but can also be made with clay. It is one of the oldest forms of art and requires great technical skill.

Inuit soapstone carvings from Canada's Nunavut Territory are subtractive sculptures.

RELIEF

Reliefs are three-dimensional images raised from the surface. A relief can be created by adding or subtracting materials from the surface. It can be done with stone or clay.

The raised writings and pictures on coins that you can feel under your fingers are created by methods of relief sculpting on plaster. The final design is then transferred onto metal coins.

CONSTRUCTION

3-D art can be constructed by joining materials together using glue or any type of fastener. 3-D artists may weld metal or nail wood forms together.

Horizontal by Alexander Calder is an example of a welded metal construction sculpture.

ASSEMBLAGE

3-D art can be created by assembling found objects together to create something new.

Tree of the Aeolian Harp, a 1992 assemblage by Lubo Kristek, was created using various pieces of metal.

MATERIALS AND TECHNIQUES

Air-drying clay and papier-mâché are used for many of the projects in this book. Air-drying clay feels like regular clay and can be molded in the same way, but does not need to be **fired** in a kiln. It dries on its own in about a day. Papier-mâché is traditionally made with flour and water, but it also can be made with a water and glue mixture that's not prone to mold or being eaten by critters.

When working with clay or papier-mâché, often a base or supporting structure is created first. Then the clay or papier-mâché is laid on top. When the base is made out of wire, it is called an armature.

Tip
Throw leftover clay in the garbage and wipe your hands well before washing them off. Clay can harden in drains!

Air-drying clay comes in white and terracotta colors.

Use lightweight aluminum craft wire for armatures. It can be cut with scissors.

Sculpting tools can be used for carving and smoothing clay. Or you can use a plastic knife instead.

WORKING WITH CLAY

Modeling clay is oily and can be messy. Prepare a work area. A piece of cardboard or foam board is great to work on, or cover a tabletop with wax paper. Wash your hands well when you finish working, as they will be oily, too.

Always start by kneading the clay in your hands to warm it up and soften it.

To form a ball, move your hands in a circle while pressing the clay lightly between them.

To make a coil shape, roll the clay on a flat surface with your fingers.

BASIC SHAPES

All of these shapes can be made big or small or thin or thick, depending on the amount of clay used and the pressure applied. Use your fingers to squish, smooth, pinch, flatten, and poke the clay into whatever shape you want.

To make a slab, start with a large piece and flatten it on your work surface. Keep pressing the clay out and away from the center until it is as flat as you want it.

PAPIER-MÂCHÉ

Papier-mâché is made of a mixture of strips of paper and glue, or paper, flour, and water. When it dries, it becomes hard. You can make all kinds of objects with papier-mâché.

Papier-mâché is really easy to do. You don't need a lot of materials. Start by preparing your glue mixture and making newspaper strips. Tear the newspaper pages into strips about 1 inch (2.5 cm) wide by 4 inches (10 cm) long. Make a big pile of strips. And now the fun begins!

PAPIER-MÂCHÉ TECHNIQUE

Before you start applying paper strips, prepare your mold and shapes for the bases. You can create forms from crumpled newspapers and cardboard products, bowls or plates, or balloons. Paper towel rolls and pipe cleaners work well, too. Balloons are great for round shapes because they will tear away from your dried papier-mâché easily when they burst. When using bowls or plates, cover them with a thin layer of Vaseline (or use petroleum jelly) to stop the papier-mâché from sticking to them.

Once your molds are ready, it is time to apply the paper strips. Cover the strips of paper with glue on both sides using a paintbrush. Then place your strips one at a time over the mold, smoothing the strips to remove any air bubbles. Cover the mold with two or three layers at a time. If you put too many layers on at once, it will take too long to dry. Build up the layers until you have the thickness you want.

When completely dry, cover your creation with two coats of paint to seal it. You can use any type of paint, but the most popular paint is water-based acrylic. It is easy to use and quick to dry.

PAPIER-MÂCHÉ GLUE

You Will Need:
- Large mixing bowl (8 cups or 1.9 L)
- 1 cup (250 mL) flour or glue
- 3 tablespoons (45 mL) salt
- 2 cups (500 mL) water
- Measuring cup
- Spoon

Made with Flour

Add flour and salt to a bowl and add water slowly, mixing with a spoon. Continue to add water until your paste is like a thin pancake batter, smooth with no lumps.

Made with Glue

Add 1 cup (250 mL) of white glue and 2 cups (500 mL) of water to a bowl. Mix together with a spoon until the mixture is well blended.

PINCHING CLAY

In this exercise you will mold and form clay into a pot. You will use a pinching technique to shape the clay. Clay is also very forgiving. If you don't like your bowl mash the clay together and start again.

You Will Need:
- Wax paper
- Air-drying clay
- Tempera or acrylic paint
- Stir stick
- Brush
- Sculpting tool or plastic knife

PROJECT GUIDES

1 Cover your work area with wax paper to protect the table surface. Make a ball out of a lump of clay. Roll it in your hands. Then roll it on your work area to smooth the clay out.

2 While holding the ball in one hand, press your thumb from your other hand into the ball. Keep pressing your thumb into the ball while moving it around to make the hole bigger. Continue pressing until you have a nice bowl shape.

3 Turn the bowl upside down and tap it on the tabletop to smooth the top of the bowl.

4 Wet the bowl with a little bit of water on your fingertips. Smooth over any cracks in the bowl with your fingertips.

5 Make a clay **slip** by mixing equal parts water and white clay in a small container. The mixture should be thick and smooth. Add a few drops of tempera or acrylic paint to the mixture. Mix together. Brush it all over the bowl and let it dry.

6 When dry, scrape away some of the colored slip. You can use a plastic knife, dull pencil, or a ribbon end sculpting tool. Make a pattern such as a zig-zag line or joined triangles. You could also make flowers. Brush the extra clay away with a dry brush.

1

2
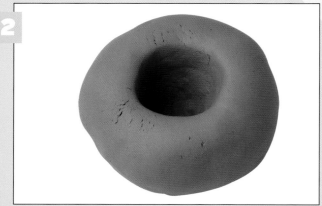

3

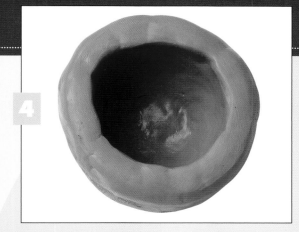

4

5

6

SGRAFITTO

Sgraffito allows an artist to create in a seemingly magical way by revealing hidden colors. In this technique, a surface is covered with one color, then a second color is applied over it. The artist scratches the top layer to create patterns using the color and texture underneath. The name sgraffito comes from the Italian word for "scratch." It's an ancient technique, but it became very popular in the 1500s and 1600s in Italy.

This sgraffito pot was made in Pennsylvania around 1835.

Try This!
Try decorating your pot by pressing beads, small stones, or other decorative items directly into the clay. Try pressing a stamp onto the clay to make decorative marks. Experiment with different ways to make marks in clay.

OUT OF THE BACKGROUND

In this exercise, you will use the subtractive technique to create a relief tile by removing portions of clay from a solid piece of clay base. A relief tile is a flat surface with a 3-D object coming out of the base. The space around the carving is **negative space** and will be removed with a sculpting tool. In this way, you transform a two-dimensional drawing into a three-dimensional piece of art. Instead of being flat, reliefs and other 3-D art take on form and volume and can look quite lifelike.

You Will Need:

- Air-drying clay
- Rolling pin
- Scissors
- Plastic knife or sculpting tool
- Paper and pencil
- Tempera or acrylic paint
- Brushes

PROJECT GUIDES

1. Use a rolling pin to roll out a ½ inch (1.3 cm) thick slab of clay. Use a plastic knife to cut out a tile shape and put the extra clay aside.

2. Cut a piece of paper the same size as your tile. Draw a gecko or other figure on the paper. Place it over the tile and trace the drawing with a pencil. This will make a slight indentation on the clay. Remove the paper.

3. Use a plastic knife or sculpting tool to remove the clay surrounding the drawing. Carve to a depth of ¼ inch (0.6 cm).

4. Wet the tile with a little bit of water on your fingertips. Smooth over the sculpture and background. With your fingertips mold the sides of the sculpture. If you remove too much clay add some back. Moisten the clay first so it will stick and press it into the sculpture. Use the knife to make decorative marks in the clay. Let it dry.

5. Paint the sculpture. Let it dry.

6. Paint fine details like eyes and spots.

Try This!

Abstract art often has no recognizable subject. You can create a relief tile by using an additive technique which adds clay to a tile. Make a thinner tile shape. Roll out another thin slab of clay. Cut out shapes. Scratch the bottom of the surface of the shapes and wet the clay slightly. Then press them into the relief tile.

4

5

6

Terracotta reliefs are one of the oldest known art forms, dating back to prehistoric times. The Romans are especially famous for reliefs, but they were also made in ancient Greece, Asia, Africa, and the Middle East.

The Romans decorated inside and outside their homes with reliefs that showed anything from grand myths to daily life. They made reliefs from a coarse clay that was cheaper and easier to use than stone or bronze. The clay takes a reddish color when dry. Both the color and clay are called terracotta. Ancient reliefs were often painted brightly, though the paint has faded over time. The art of terracotta relief faded, too, as the Roman Empire ended, but it was revived during the Renaissance, often for religious art.

Part of a roman relief sculpture from around the first century shows figures from mythology.

RAISED SURFACES

Construct a high-relief artwork using felt, fabric, and cardboard. In this exercise, you will be adding and building up to create the relief. You will also be creating a 3-D effect by having the foreground raised and closer to the viewer than the distant background. This is a 3-D **collage** created with fabric rather than paper. The texture of the fabric adds visual interest to the artwork.

You Will Need:
- Photo
- Pencil
- Cardboard
- Art board (canvas board or cardboard)
- Fabric scraps
- Glue that dries clear
- Brush

PROJECT GUIDES

1 Choose a reference photo of a **landscape**.

2 Break the reference photo into shapes. Draw the shapes onto a piece of cardboard. The cardboard should be as wide as your art board. Cut the shapes out.

3 Decide what color of fabric scraps to use. Cut the fabric scraps to be just slightly larger than the cardboard pieces.

4 Brush glue over a cardboard piece. Press and smooth the fabric into the glue. Fold the fabric over the edge and glue to the back. Continue until all the cardboard pieces have been covered with fabric.

5 Cover the top of the art board with glue. Lay fabric pieces on the art board to create the sky and smooth out.

6 Glue the first piece of fabric-covered cardboard to the art board. For each new fabric-covered layer you add, first add a strip of cardboard underneath it as support. Continue this process until the art board is covered.

7 Glue the final pieces such as trees and, in this case, the bear, to the art board.

1

2

3

Cardboard support piece

JOYCE WIELAND

(1930–1988) Canada

Joyce Wieland experimented with all kinds of art forms, including painting, sculpture, film, and fabric arts. To decorate a subway station, she chose a traditional scene showing Canadian caribou. Then she created the large wall hanging as a showcase for the traditional women's arts of quilting and **applique**.

Barren Ground Caribou, a fabric installation by Joyce Wieland at Spadina subway station in Toronto, was created in 1978.

13

SHAPING CLAY

Clay has many uses in art because it is soft and easy to shape. That same softness, though, means that additive clay sculptures may need a frame to hold them up. Wire frames like the one in this project are often found in **scale models** for larger works, which are called maquettes. Maquette is a French word meaning scale model.

PROJECT GUIDES

1 Make a loop with your piece of wire. Bend it to make an interesting form.

2 Make some shapes from the clay. Roll out some clay with your fingers until it becomes a thin coil. Roll clay in your hands to create small balls.

3 Make a slab of clay about 3 inches (7.6 cm) wide and 2 inches (5 cm) tall to use as the base of the sculpture. Smooth the edges. Press the joined ends of the wire loop into the clay. Wrap clay coils around the wire frame.

4 Wet the clay slightly and start to blend the coils together. Add the balls of clay and press into the form. Twist the wire and clay to create a shape you like.

5 Add more clay and smooth all the edges where clay has been added. Use a little bit of water on your fingertips to wet the clay which helps blend the clay together. You can also rub a sculpting tool over the clay to smooth out the joined areas of the clay. Leave overnight to dry.

6 Paint the sculpture with metallic paint to mimic the look of a bronze sculpture. Paint the base with black paint.

1
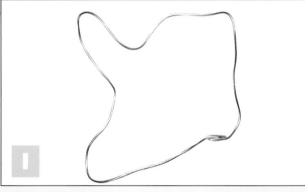

2
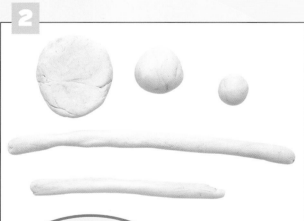

Did You Know?

Maquettes are often used to show how the full-size public sculpture will look and fit into its space. Michelangelo always made a clay or wax maquette before creating a full-size sculpture.

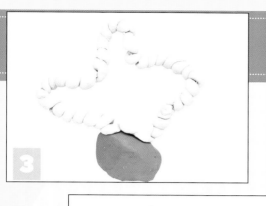

3

4

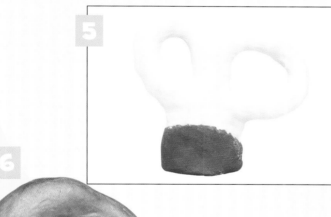

5

6

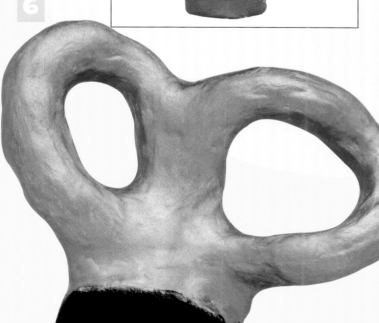

(1898–1986) England

Henry Moore became famous for sculpting semi-abstract human forms with bumps, hollows, and even holes in them. He was inspired by forms and shapes in nature. These included hills and valleys, and items he gathered on his walks outdoors, such as stones, shells, and roots.

Many of Moore's sculptures are massive works of public art in bronze, marble, stone, wood, or even brick. But he usually started out with clay maquettes, some so small he could hold them in his hand. He had a special studio just for maquette making!

Large Two Forms (1969), a bronze sculpture by Henry Moore, is pictured here in front of the Art Gallery of Ontario in Toronto.

ART IN GEOMETRY

Many sculptures are an **organic** form. They are full of curves and smooth surfaces. But you can also make a sculpture from **geometric** shapes. When you combine four triangles together you get a tetrahedron or triangular pyramid. This can be the base for an amazing sculpture composed only of triangles.

You Will Need:

- Air-drying clay (white or colored)
- Toothpicks, both ends pointed
- Glue
- Tempera paint for white clay

PROJECT GUIDES

1 If you have colored clay you can skip this step. Divide your clay into three pieces. Add a few drops of tempera paint onto the first piece. Mix the clay and paint together. Wash your hands. Repeat with the other two pieces.

2 Make tiny balls of clay (slightly bigger than a pea) from each piece of colored clay.

3 Take three of the balls. Arrange the toothpicks and balls into a triangle shape. Poke each end of a toothpick into a clay ball.

4 Take three more toothpicks and poke each end into the clay balls in the formed triangle. Push them toward the center and add a clay ball to cover the ends. You have now created a tetrahedron.

5 Create a base by adding more triangles and tetrahedrons to the first one. Poke toothpicks into the clay balls. Join those toothpicks together with another clay ball to form a new triangle. Repeat, always attaching the new triangle to an existing one.

6 Start building up and making the structure taller. Start adding triangles to the clay balls on top.

7 Continue building until you are happy with your sculpture. Try to finish with a triangle on top.

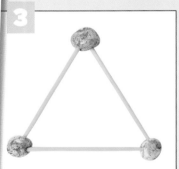

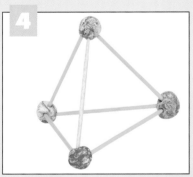

Tip

As your structure gets bigger some toothpicks may pop out of the clay. Use a toothpick dipped in glue to dab a bit of glue around the toothpick where it meets the clay.

Try This!

Try building a big sculpture with a group of friends. How tall a structure can you make? As you build keep checking to make sure it is stable. The taller the structure, the bigger the base it will need.

First tetrahedron

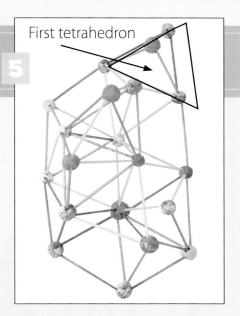

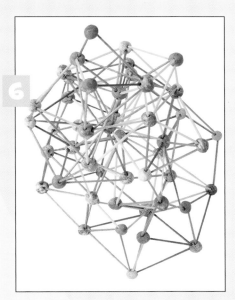

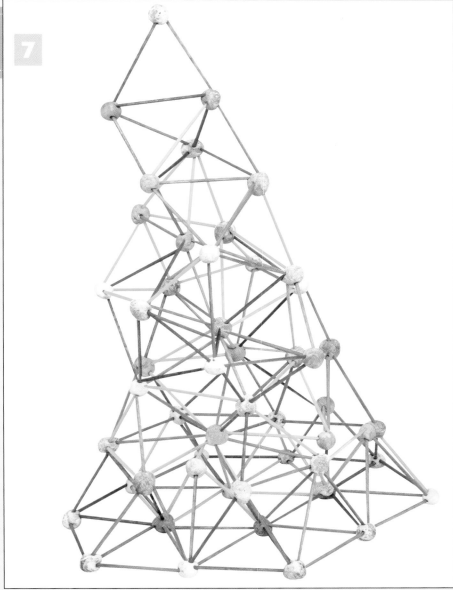

GEORGE W. HART

(1955) United States

George W. Hart found geometry so interesting, and so much fun, that he became a math professor. He shares his love of geometry by making it into art. He creates **polyhedrons** from all kinds of objects that are hooked, glued, and screwed together. One of his works used apples and oranges to have some fun with the old saying that you can't mix the two. Another, made for a library, used 60 books that he had read. He creates toys and puzzles, too.

George W. Hart displays one of his sculpture puzzles.

PAPER SCULPTURES

Making small models out of wire and paper is another way artists can experiment before creating a large sculpture out of steel. Steel is often used for public works of art because it can withstand the elements. Steel can be painted, making it an ideal material for colorful sculptures.

You Will Need:

- Colored card stock
- Pencil
- Scissors
- 10 mm wire
- Masking tape
- Glue
- Foam or cardboard
- Palette or plastic knife
- Paint and brush

PROJECT GUIDES

1. Make an abstract model of a person or animal using shapes. Decide on shapes that stack well. They could be crescents as in the example, or circles or triangles. Draw them on one piece of colored card stock and cut them out. Turn the shapes over, trace around them and cut a second set of shapes out.

2. Lay one set of shapes out. Use scissors to cut a piece of wire a little shorter than the length of the figure. Cut another piece a little shorter than the width of the figure. Cut a third piece a little longer than the bottom of the figure. Tape the wires to the shapes.

3. Cover the wire on the shapes completely with tape.

4. Cover these shapes with glue. Lay the second set of shapes on top. The wire is now in the middle. Smooth and press together while keeping the edges **aligned**.

5. Repeat steps 1 to 4 to make additional shapes to go beside the main sculpture.

6. Make a base by painting a rectangular piece of cardboard. Let it dry.

7. Poke the ends of the wire that extend from the shapes through the base. Bend the wire and tape it to the bottom of the base. Adjust the sculptures by bending them.

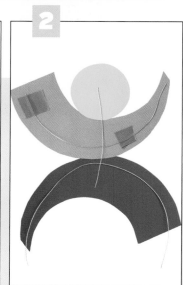

5

6

Try This!

Take a photo of your completed sculpture. Take a photo of a city landmark, such as your school, a library, or town hall. Use a photo app to remove the background from the sculpture photo. Paste it into the city photo and make the sculpture larger so you can see how your sculpture would look as a public work of art.

7

Tip

If you don't have colored card stock you can paint poster board with tempera or acrylic paint. Leave it to dry and then cut out your shapes.

ALEXANDER CALDER

(1898–1976) United States

Alexander Calder always liked making things. As a child, he made toys from wire, cloth, and string. He studied engineering and worked as a mechanic before becoming an artist like his grandfather and mother. Calder was fascinated with the way things move. He began making large public sculptures called stabiles that looked like they were moving. Calder used basic shapes and brightly colored metal to appeal to all ages.

Calder's sculptures are eye-catching.

19

WIRED CREATURE

Some large-scale public sculptures are of small objects, animals, or insects enlarged to be gigantic. Think of a sculpture you could make of a winged creature. You will use wire to create the base of the model. When the sculpture is complete, think about what materials could be used to make a large version and where it could be displayed.

You Will Need:

- 10 mm wire
- Scissors
- Papier-mâché glue
- Thin paper towel
- Tissue paper
- Markers
- Plastic wrap
- Foam or cardboard

PROJECT GUIDES

1. Decide on the size of the creature you will make. Use scissors to cut a piece of wire, it should be about double the size of your finished sculpture. Fold it in half making a loop at one end. Twist the two ends of the wire together. This is the body.

2. Cut two more equal lengths of wire to make wings. They should be five times bigger than the size you want one wing to be. Fold one piece of wire in half. Twist the two ends together, leaving about 2 inches (5 cm) of extra wire. Press the middle of the loop down to where the wire is joined. Wrap some of the extra wire around the center of the loop. Repeat with the other wire.

3. Cut three small pieces of wire for legs. Bend each in half.

4. Put some papier-mâché glue in a plastic container. (See page 7.) Put a strip of paper towel into the glue. Remove the excess glue with your fingers. Wrap the paper towel around the wire body. Attach the wings by wrapping the wire ends around the body. Attach the legs by placing them over the body and then twisting the wire to secure them.

5. Tear small pieces of tissue paper. Press them onto the body. Dab more glue on the body. Do the same for the legs. Put glue on the wire and then cover with the tissue paper. Make two small balls of dark-colored tissue paper, dip them in glue and press to the head. Color the wire wings with a marker.

6. Cut pieces of plastic wrap slightly bigger than the wings. Wrap it around the wings, tucking the extra plastic wrap underneath the wire. Use markers to color the wings.

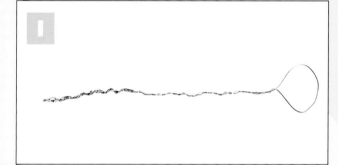

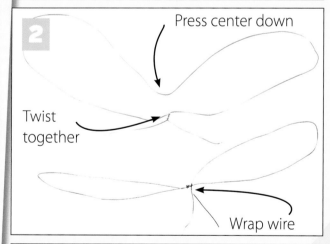

Press center down

Twist together

Wrap wire

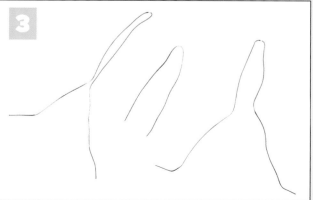

4

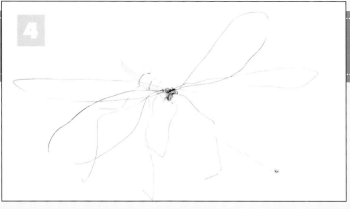

5

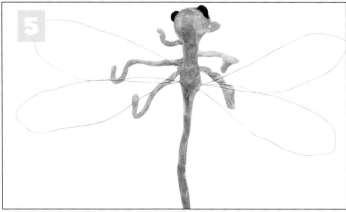

6

(1911–2010) France/United States

Painter and sculptor Louise Bourgeois suffered many troubles, including her mother's death, while growing up. She used her art to express her experiences and help her cope. She found comfort in all of nature, even spiders, which she saw as protective, strong, and clever, like her mother. She is famous for a 30-foot-tall (9 m) steel sculpture of a spider called *Maman*, which means mother in French. Bourgeois made sculptures from wood, steel, stone, wire, and even her own old clothes.

Maman was created in 1999 from stainless steel, bronze, and marble.

PROJECT GUIDES
CONTINUED

7 Cut a piece of cardboard or Styrofoam slightly larger than your sculpture. This will be the base. Spread glue over the base and cover with torn pieces of tissue paper. Glue the feet of the creature to the base.

ART IN THE SKY

Create a sculpture of a bird using the technique of papier-mâché. For this larger project, you will use a pop bottle, a balloon, and cardboard items to make a sturdy base for your 3-D art. This example shows how to create a goose, but you can modify the instructions to create any bird.

You Will Need:

- Pressed paperboard or thin cardboard
- Scissors
- Tape
- Large pop bottle
- Paper towel tube
- Newspapers
- Small balloon
- Cardboard egg carton
- Papier-mâché glue
- Acrylic or tempera paint
- Brush
- Hook and wire or string

PROJECT GUIDES

1 Choose the subject for the sculpture. Find photos of the subject for reference.

2 Cut two wing shapes from paperboard or cardboard.

3 Tape the two wings to the top of the pop bottle. Fill a paper towel tube with scrunched up newspaper. Put one end over the open end of the pop bottle. Tape in place.

4 Blow up a small balloon. Cut out an egg carton divider to make the beak. Tape the egg carton piece to the balloon.

5 Tape the head to the end of the paper towel tube.

6 Cut two webbed feet from cardboard. Tape them to the bottom of the pop bottle. Tape two bunches of scrunched up newspaper to the bottle just above the feet.

7 Tear strips of newspaper. Prepare a container of papier-mâché glue. (See page 7.) Dip a strip into the glue, then use your fingers to squeeze off the extra glue. Wrap the strip around the bottom of the bird's body. Continue dipping the strips and wrapping them around the body until the entire bird is covered. Make sure to overlap and change directions of the strips as you work. Smooth the surface with your hands to make sure there are no air bubbles. Let it dry.

8 Paint your sculpture. When dry, screw a hook into the body and hang it.

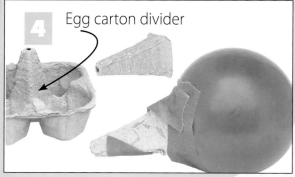

Egg carton divider

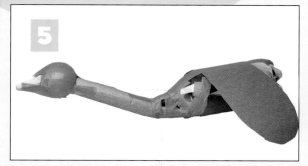

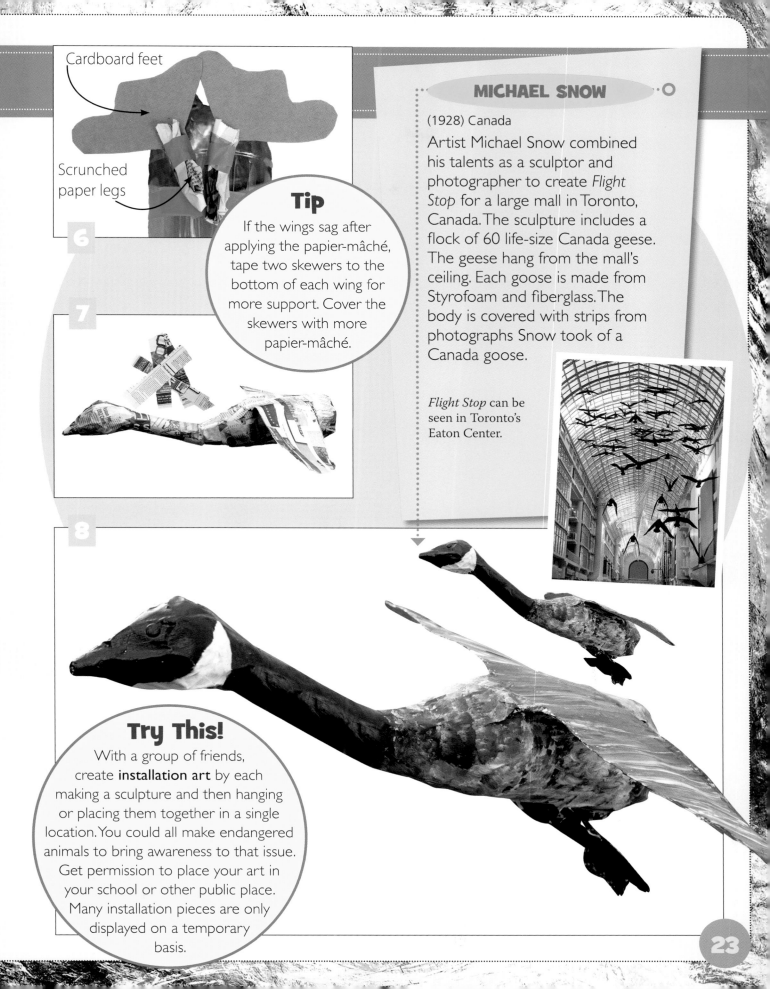

Cardboard feet

Scrunched
paper legs

6

7

Tip

If the wings sag after applying the papier-mâché, tape two skewers to the bottom of each wing for more support. Cover the skewers with more papier-mâché.

8

Try This!

With a group of friends, create **installation art** by each making a sculpture and then hanging or placing them together in a single location. You could all make endangered animals to bring awareness to that issue. Get permission to place your art in your school or other public place. Many installation pieces are only displayed on a temporary basis.

MICHAEL SNOW

(1928) Canada

Artist Michael Snow combined his talents as a sculptor and photographer to create *Flight Stop* for a large mall in Toronto, Canada. The sculpture includes a flock of 60 life-size Canada geese. The geese hang from the mall's ceiling. Each goose is made from Styrofoam and fiberglass. The body is covered with strips from photographs Snow took of a Canada goose.

Flight Stop can be seen in Toronto's Eaton Center.

THAT'S ART, FOLKS

In this exercise, you will create a piece of folk art. In coastal communities where fishing is very important, brightly decorated fish are often created from driftwood, found on coastal beaches. You will create the look of a wooden fish using papier-mâché. Papier-mâché can be made using any type of paper. In this case paper towel will be used because it creates interesting textures and provides a white base.

PROJECT GUIDES

1. Draw a fish shape about the size of your hand on a blank piece of paper. Cut it out. Use the paper cut-out as a pattern. Place it on the cardboard and trace around it. Flip it over so the fish faces the opposite direction and trace around it again.

2. Use scissors to cut out both fish.

3. Tape a craft stick to the back of one of the cardboard fish.

4. Spread glue all over one of the cardboard fish. Place the other cardboard fish on top and press them together. Crumple up some paper. Glue the crumpled paper to both sides of the fish to create round sides. Poke the craft stick into your block of Styrofoam.

5. Prepare some papier-mâché glue (see page 7). Tear paper towels into thin strips. Dip a paper towel strip into the glue. Pull the strip through two fingers to remove excess glue. Wrap the strip around the fish. Repeat this until the fish is completely covered. Let it dry.

6. Paint the fish with bright colors. Make patterns. Paint the Styrofoam block. Let it dry.

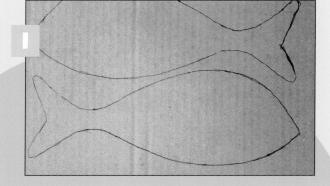

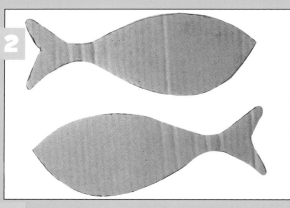

Did You Know?

Some areas become known for one special type of folk art, such as the decorative fish that are made along the east coast of North America.

4

5

Folk art is often used for decorative purposes. It is made from natural resources found in an area. For example, weaving uses thread dyed from plants in the area. Folk art is often based on simple shapes and is usually very colorful. It can be made from cloth, wood, clay, metal, stone, or paper.

Examples of Mexican folk art

6

Try This!

Find a piece of driftwood, if you live near a body of water, or a weathered piece of wood. Paint a fish or other subject directly on the wood. Have an adult attach a picture hanger to the back and hang it on your wall.

NATURE YARN

Make a sculpture from a tree branch by covering it with scraps of yarn. In this fun and easy project you will learn how to transform any ordinary tree branch into a unique piece of art. Use many different colors of yarn to make your project visually interesting.

PROJECT GUIDES

1. Find a small tree branch. Often they will be lying on the ground in parks.

2. You will use clay to make a vase for your branch. Roll a small slab of clay into a cylinder shape. Press your thumb into the center to make an opening at the top. Dip your fingertips in water and smooth out the clay. Make sure there are no cracks.

3. Push the end of the branch into the clay vase. Let it dry. It will be easier to wrap the branch with it supported in the vase.

4. Take a long piece of yarn, about 36 inches (91 cm) long, and tie it to the bottom of one twig. The amount of yarn it takes will depend on the thickness of the wool and the length of the branch. If you run out of yarn while wrapping, cut another piece of yarn and tie it to the first piece, then continue wrapping.

5. Start wrapping the yarn around the twig. Pull it tight as you wrap. When you get to the end, tie a knot. Leave the loose ends until later.

6. Cover each twig and the rest of the branch with yarn. Put some glue on each knot. When the glue is dry, trim the ends of the yarn.

7. Paint the vase. Use the tip of the paint brush to paint dots.

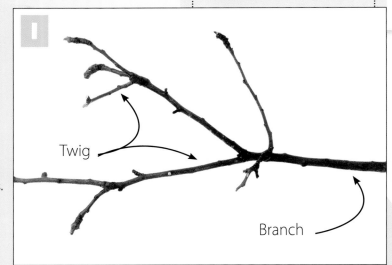

1 Twig ← → Branch →

2

3

Try This!

With a group of friends, try covering something larger than a tree branch. Wrap yarn around objects such as a chair or the legs of a desk or table.

YARN BOMBING

Yarn bombing, also called graffiti knitting, is a new kind of folk art. Yarn bombers cover park benches, lampposts, statues, tree trunks, and even buses with knitting or crochet. No one knows for sure where it started, but it has spread worldwide. At first, yarn bombers always struck in secret. They still do, but there are also official yarn-bombing projects in some towns! Either way, the goal is simple: to brighten up the world, and make people smile.

Ohio yarn bombers wrapped trees to say thank you to them.

ASSEMBLING ART

Assemblage comes from the word assemble, and that's what it is: putting things together in a new way to make art. For this project, you will create an animal using found objects from around the house, such as clean cans from the recycling bin, cardboard spools, straws, and buttons. Look for interesting shapes and textures. Choose any animal you would like. Think about your animal's coloring and features as you gather your objects.

You Will Need:
- Clean cans
- Other assorted junk
- Glue
- Permanent markers

PROJECT GUIDES

1. You will need found objects from around the house to form the following parts of your animal:
   - body
   - legs
   - neck
   - head
   - face—eyes, nose, mouth, and ears

2. To start, you will need the objects you have chosen for your animal's body and its legs. In this example, the cat's body is a tin can and four cardboard spools form its legs. Glue the legs to the body so the sculpture can stand up on its own.

3. Next, glue your animal's neck to its body. Let it dry before gluing the head to the neck.

4. Next, you will add features to your animal's face, including eyes, ears, a nose, and mouth. Depending on the animal you chose, you may also need to add whiskers, a mane, or other features specific to your animal sculpture.

5. Your animal's tail is next. What materials did you choose? The tail shown here was made from a piece of leather cord. The cord was tied in knots and glued to the body.

6. Color the can with permanent markers. You may add any materials you gathered for your animal's covering.

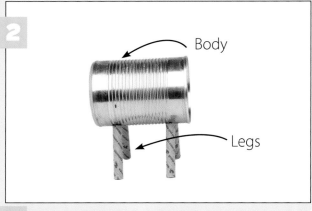

Body

Legs

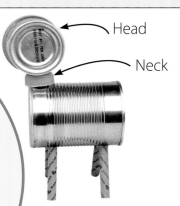

Head

Neck

Tip

You can use regular glue for this project. Use blobs of it rather than a little drop. A low-temperature glue gun would work very well for this project as well.

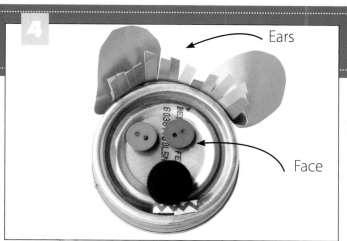

4

Ears

Face

5

Tail

6

ROBERT RAUSCHENBERG

(1925-2008) United States

Artist Robert Rauschenberg worked in many mediums including painting, sculpture, prints, and photography. He was also well known for assemblage art. He wanted to show that art can be anywhere—and anything. He called his works "combines" because they combined sculpture and painting, often using found objects.

American artist Robert Rauschenberg turned old bikes into this sculpture called *Riding Bikes* in 1998.

LEARNING MORE

Books

3-D Art Lab for Kids,
by Susan Schwake, Quarry Books, 2013.

Clay Lab for Kids,
by Cassie Stephens, Quarry Books, 2017.

Usborne Book of Papier Mache
by Ray Gibson, Usborne Publishing, 1995.

Three-Dimensional Art Adventures
by Maja Pitamic and Jill Laidlaw, Chicago Review Press, 2016.

Websites

National Gallery of Art
www.nga.gov/education/kids.html
NGAkids Art Zone includes descriptions of interactive art-making tools that are free to download. You can also explore the collection at the National Gallery.

All about Alexander Calder
www.tate.org.uk/art/artists/alexander-calder-848/who-is-alexander-calder
Learn more about Alexander Calder at the Tate Gallery, including Calder-inspired art projects.

Top 5 Sculptures
www.tate.org.uk/kids/explore/top-5/top-5-sculptures
A great introduction to sculpture as well as a wonderful collection of quizzes, art activities, and artist's bios.

Everything You Ever Wanted to Know About Clay
https://kinderart.com/art-lessons/sculpture/about-clay/
This website features tools and techniques for working with clay.

GLOSSARY

abstract art Art that can be made from lines, shapes, and colors that do not represent an actual form but convey emotion

aligned Properly positioned with relationship to one another; often in a line

applique Decorative needlework in which pieces of fabric are used to form pictures or patterns

collage A piece of art that combines various materials and media

dimensions A measurable extent of some kind, such as height, width, and depth

fired Art term for baked in a high-temperature oven

geometric A word to describe shapes such as circles, triangles, or squares that have perfect form and don't often appear in nature

High Renaissance The time from the 1490s to 1527, when the great masters Leonardo da Vinci, Michelangelo, and Raphael all were at work

installation art A style of art that features a group of 3-D art forms in an indoor location such as a museum, mall, or library

kiln A large, hot oven that is used to fire the clay

landscape A painting or photo where the subject is nature, usually mountains, forests, oceans, lakes, rivers, trees, and valleys

negative space The space around and between subjects of an artwork or photo

organic A word to describe shapes and forms associated with the natural world that are not geometric

polyhedron A solid figure with many sides

scale model A physical representation of an object, usually smaller, but with the same key elements in the same relationship

sgraffito A decorating technique used in pottery. One color layer is scratched away to reveal a bottom layer in a different color.

slip Clay with a lot of water added to it, often used as a sort of glue to hold clay pieces together

techniques The ways in which things are done to accomplish a goal

terracotta A reddish brown clay-like earth, or the color itself; the name comes from the Italian words for "baked earth"

weld To unite metals by heating so that they flow together

INDEX

ABOUT THE AUTHOR

Jane Yates studied art at OCAD, and Ryerson University. She worked as a freelance photographer before shifting to children's publishing where she's worked as a designer, writer, editor, and creative director. Combining her vast experience in children's publishing and her love for arts and crafts, Yates has authored over 20 craft books for children. Yates shares her home with her family, two giant dogs, and an attack cat.